CHRISTOPHER CHURCHMOUSE CLASSICS®

THE TATTLETALE TONGUE

"If your brother sins, go and reprove him in private"—Matthew 18:15.

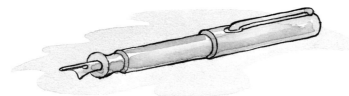

WRITTEN BY BARBARA DAVOLL
Pictures by Dennis Hockerman

A Sonflower Book

VICTOR BOOKS®
A DIVISION OF SCRIPTURE PRESS PUBLICATIONS INC.
USA CANADA ENGLAND

CHRISTOPHER CHURCHMOUSE CLASSICS

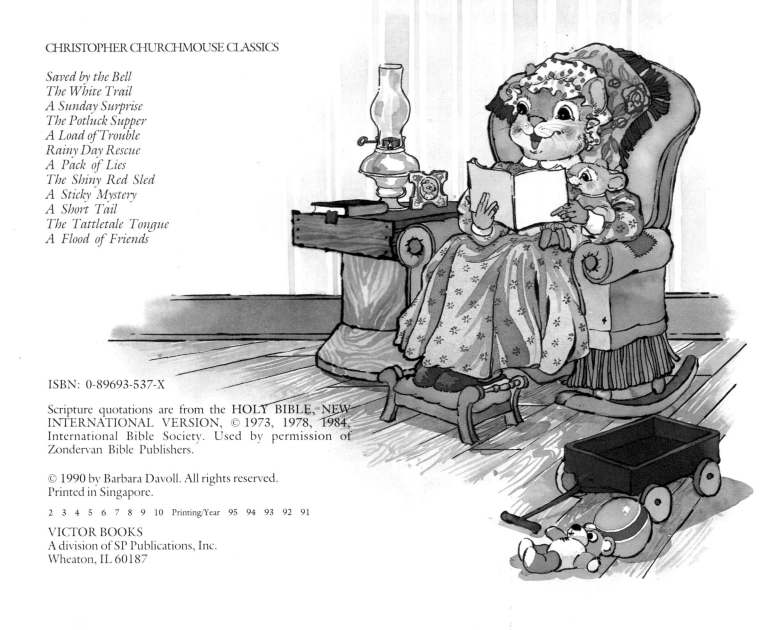

ISBN: 0-89693-537-X

Scripture quotations are from the HOLY BIBLE, NEW INTERNATIONAL VERSION, © 1973, 1978, 1984, International Bible Society. Used by permission of Zondervan Bible Publishers.

2 3 4 5 6 7 8 9 10 Printing/Year 95 94 93 92 91

VICTOR BOOKS
A division of SP Publications, Inc.
Wheaton, IL 60187

A Word to Parents and Teachers

The Christopher Churchmouse Series will help children grow in their knowledge of the Lord as they hear about a delightful mouse and his family and friends.

The Tattletale Tongue is one of these character-building stories. Children will learn what God says about tattling:

> *"If your brother sins, go and reprove him in private"*
> —Matthew 18:15 (NASB).

> *"The tongue is a small part of the body, and yet it boasts of great things"*
> —James 3:5 (NASB).

This book describes how Christopher jumped to conclusions and got one of his best friends in great trouble.

The Discussion Starters on page 24 can help children make practical application of the biblical truths. Happy reading!

Christopher's Friend,

Barbara Davoll

Tilly Teacher stood on the steps of the schoolhouse and rang the bell to call the mice children into school. They trooped in noisily, carrying books and lunch buckets, laughing and talking together. Soon they were settled at their desks as Miss Tilly called each name.

"Mandy Mouse," said Miss Tilly.

"Here," said Mandy.

"Freddie Fieldmouse," continued Miss Tilly.

"Here," answered Freddie.

"Sed Churchmouse," said Miss Tilly.

There was no answer. Miss Tilly looked up in surprise as Freddie ex-plained, "Sed and Ted aren't here, Miss Tilly."

"Why, that's unusual," said Miss Tilly. "I've never known those mice boys to miss school. I wonder—"

Just then the door burst open and Sed and Ted ran in, dropping their books and homework papers. "Good—good morning, Miss Tilly," Ted gasped, scrambling on the floor to pick up the mess.

"I'm sorry we're late, but we had a problem at home," explained Sed, helping Ted pick up some books.

"Well, sometimes things do happen," soothed Miss Tilly. "I hope it wasn't a serious problem."

"Well, uh, I guess it is serious. You see, my mother's gold pen has been lost, and she's awfully upset. Ever since we got up this morning we've been looking for it."

"Oh, my!" exclaimed Miss Tilly. "I'm sure Aunt Snootie is very sad. I know how much that pen meant to her. I believe her father got it from a very wealthy home where he lived. What do you think could have happened to it, boys?"

Sed and Ted looked very ashamed as Ted answered in a low voice, "She—she thinks it was stolen by one of the young mice."

"Stolen!? Why, I'm sure none of our mice would do such a thing!" Miss Tilly thought a moment. "And just to prove it, we're going to clean this schoolroom. I want all of you to search your desks. Put everything out on top so that I may see. They need a good cleaning anyway. I'll clean my desk too."

6

Soon there was a lot of talking in that room. "Hey! Look what I found!" cried Freddie Fieldmouse. "Last week's homework assignment I thought I lost!" He waved a bent-up piece of paper.

"Ooo, yuk," groaned Christopher Churchmouse in disgust, pulling out a moldy half-eaten sandwich from his desk. "Look at this."

"Mmm, Chris, nice lunch you've got there," snickered one of the mice boys.

"Have a bite," Christopher laughed, waving it toward the boy's nose.

"I found my book I lost last month!" cried Mandy Mouse.

The mice cleaned and searched for the pen nearly all day. At last it was time to go home.

"Whew," muttered Freddie Fieldmouse to Christopher. "That was some day. I'm exhausted!"

"Me too," said Christopher. Then he laughed and wiped off a big smudge on Freddie's face. "It looks like you're wearing half the dirt home, Freddie!"

9

When Christopher got home, Mama had his favorite cookies waiting. He sat down and told her all about his day.

"That's too bad," said Mama sympathetically, sitting down at the table with Christopher. "I was with Aunt Snootie this afternoon trying to help her think of all the places she could have left that pen herself."

"Well, I think it's terrible," fussed Christopher, taking a big bite of his second cookie.

"What's terrible, Christopher?"

"The way Aunt Snootie is accusing all of us mice of stealing her pen.

Who would want her old pen anyway? I'll bet it's not even gold."

"Christopher!" said Mama. "It's very important to Aunt Snootie, whatever it's made of."

"Yes, Mama."

10

That evening Christopher went to Sed's home to play. They were all settled upstairs playing checkers when Uncle Rootie called Sed.

"Coming!" Sed called back. He looked at Christopher. "I'll be right back. Don't you cheat while I'm gone!"

"I won't!" laughed Christopher. He watched Sed run down the stairs, then he looked around the room. *Maybe I should look for Aunt Snootie's pen here while I'm waiting.* He walked stealthily over to Sed's desk. *There's nothing wrong with just poking around to see what I can find.* He looked over his shoulder to make sure Sed wasn't coming back yet, then turned over a couple of papers that were on the desk.

What! There was Aunt Snootie's pen! Christopher picked it up—and then dropped it as if it were a hot coal.

Didn't Sed know the pen was there? He must know! Oh, my, Christopher thought, *Sed must have stolen his own mother's pen! He usually needs a pen. He's always losing his.* Suddenly he heard Sed starting up the stairs. Christopher pushed the papers back over the pen and sat down before the checkerboard.

"Did you cheat?" asked Sed.

"I told you I wouldn't!" answered Christopher, giving Sed a long, hard look. *Could Sed actually have stolen something from his own mother?*

The next day Christopher was walking to school with his friend Freddie Fieldmouse. "I sure hope today's a better day than yesterday," said Freddie.

"It will be. We won't have to look for that old pen again," said Christopher. He continued softly, "Freddie, I've got a secret to tell you—but you've got to promise not to tell anybody."

"I promise."

"I could get in big trouble if you tell." Giving a look in both directions to be sure no one was listening, Christopher whispered into Freddie's ear.

"What!?" shrieked Freddie excitedly.

"Shhh!" hissed Christopher with alarm. "Someone will hear us and wonder what we're talking about."

"Are you sure he stole it?"

"Well, I saw it, right on his desk."

At recess that day Christopher and a couple of his other friends were playing together when Mandy Mouse came over to join them. She was carrying a small bag of candy.

"What do you have in there, Mandy?" Christopher asked with interest.

"Some candy," mumbled Mandy, with her mouth full of the delicious stuff.

"May I have a piece, please?" begged Christopher.

"I only have two more," Mandy said reluctantly.

"I'll tell you a secret if you'll give me a piece," promised Christopher.

"Is it a good secret?"

"Oh, yes—I know who stole Aunt Snootie's pen!"

Mandy's eyes got big and round, and she handed Christopher a piece of candy as she listened. "Who ever would think that!" she exclaimed.

"Think what?" questioned a cute little girl mouse coming up behind Mandy.

"Oh, can't tell you," said Mandy smugly. "It's a secret!"

"See that you *don't*," warned Christopher as he joined the mice boys again.

The next day at school the little mice were in an uproar. It seemed that all of the mice knew Sed had stolen his mother's pen and were standing around talking about it. Whenever Sed came near, they stopped.

At lunchtime Sed went home and didn't come back. Several of the mice children in the yard began to tease his brother Ted. "Hey, Ted, where's your big brother? Gone out to steal something else?"

"You all be quiet," screamed Ted. "My brother is not a thief!"

Christopher and Freddie watched Ted out the window. "I'm sorry for him, Chris," said Freddie sadly.

"Yes, I am too," agreed Christopher. "It must be really hard when your own brother does something like that."

That evening Christopher was doing his homework when Aunt Snootie bustled in to see Mama. "I just had to stop by and tell you that I have found my gold pen!" cried Aunt Snootie with excitement.

"Why, that's wonderful!" said Mama. "Wherever did you find it?"

"Well, I remembered I was helping Sed with his homework in his room. I looked, and there it was under some papers on his desk—just where I had left it! I'm sorry if I caused you any trouble," gushed Aunt Snootie on her way out the door. "You know my father gave it to me."

Christopher sat frozen in horror as he watched Aunt Snootie leave.

"Aunt Snootie has found her pen, Christopher!" said Papa. "Did you hear her?"

17

"Yes, I heard," said Christopher with a sickly tone.

"Isn't that wonderful?" enthused Mama.

"Yes, really wonderful," murmured Chris in a flat voice. He trudged to his room.

The whole school would know tomorrow! He had misjudged his cousin and told the mice that Sed was a thief! Christopher laid his head down on his desk and began to cry.

"Why, Son, is your homework that hard?" asked Papa from the doorway.

Christopher jumped at his voice. "N—no," he sobbed. "Oh, Papa! I've done a terrible bad thing!" And he explained it all to him.

Just then a knock came at the door. Papa went to answer it. Christopher peeked from his room. "Good evening, Uncle Rootie. Won't you come in? What can I do for you?"

"I'm not sure," said Uncle Rootie in a very stern voice. "My boys tell me that Christopher has been spreading lies in school that Sed is a thief.

I understand that Sed was so hurt and embarrassed that he couldn't even go back to school after lunch."

"Yes, Chris was just telling me what happened. May I say how sorry I am. I will make sure that Christopher makes it right at school."

"Very well," said Uncle Rootie in a strained voice, shaking Papa's paw.

When the door closed, Papa motioned Christopher into the living room.

"But, Papa, I didn't tell the whole school. I just told Freddie and Mandy, and I told them not to tell."

"Sit down beside me, and let's talk," said Papa, patting the sofa beside him.

"Do you remember the verse the children's Sunday School teacher was teaching the other day about the tongue?"

"I guess I don't," admitted Christopher.

"She said the Bible says in James 3:5, 'The tongue is a small part of our body, but it makes great boasts.'"

"Our tongues *are* small," said Chris, trying to stick his out far enough to see it.

"Yes, that's right," agreed Papa. "The tongue is small, but the verse says it makes great boasts. That means it can cause a lot of hurt and pain. I think we've seen tonight just how much harm it can cause, haven't we?"

Christopher looked at Papa with big tearful eyes and nodded his head. "Oh, yes, Papa, and I am so sorry."

Papa wiped a tear from Christopher's cheek and said, "If we can't say something nice about someone, we probably shouldn't say anything at all. The Bible also says that when we have a problem with someone, we should go right to them first about it. If you had gone to Sed and asked him about the pen, this would never have happened."

"I know, Papa," said the sad little mouse.

"Chris, let's go to Sed's home tonight so you can ask his forgiveness. Then tomorrow you must go to school and tell your whole class what you have done and how sorry you are. That is the only way to make it right."

"Oh, Papa, that will be very hard," cried Christopher.

"I know it will be, Son, but that is using your tongue the right way."

And Christopher learned that night how to use his tongue. It was a lesson he would never forget.

DISCUSSION STARTERS

1. What were all of the mice upset about?
2. Why was the pen so important to Aunt Snootie?
3. Who was the first person to find the pen, and where did he find it?
4. What did Christopher think when he found the pen, and whom did he tell?
5. Why didn't Sed come back to school after lunch?
6. What should Christopher have done when he found the pen?
7. How did Christopher straighten things out with Sed and at school?